CW00386508

20 JAZZ GREATS
Playalong *for* Alto Saxophone

Bésame Mucho 8

Fever 6

Fly Me To The Moon
(In Other Words) 11

Flying Home 16

God Bless' The Child 14

Harlem Nocturne 19

Hit The Road Jack 22

I Wish I Knew How It Would
Feel To Be Free 24

I'm Gettin' Sentimental
Over You 28

Is You Is Or Is You Ain't
My Baby? 26

Jump, Jive An' Wail 31

Li'l Darlin' 34

Mas Que Nada 37

Perdido 40

Perhaps, Perhaps, Perhaps
(Quizas, Quizas, Quizas) 42

Satin Doll 44

Straight No Chaser 46

Sway (Quien Sera) 48

Take The 'A' Train 50

The Girl From Ipanema
(Garota De Ipanema) 53

Saxophone Fingering Chart 3

CD#1 - mellow

CD#2 - Upbeat

WISE PUBLICATIONS
London/New York/Paris/Sydney/Copenhagen/Madrid/Tokyo

Exclusive Distributors:
Music Sales Limited
8/9 Frith Street, London W1D 3JB, England.
Music Sales Pty Limited
120 Rothschild Avenue, Rosebery, NSW 2018, Australia.

Order No. AM970464
ISBN 0-7119-8854-4
This book © Copyright 2001 by Wise Publications.

Music arranged by Paul Honey and Jack Long.
Music processed by Enigma Music Production Services.
Cover photography by George Taylor.
Printed in Malta by Interprint Limited.

CDs produced by Paul Honey.
Instrumental solos by John Whelan.
Engineered by Kester Sims.

Your Guarantee of Quality:
As publishers, we strive to produce every book to the highest commercial
standards. This book has been carefully designed to minimise awkward page
turns and to make playing from it a real pleasure.
Particular care has been given to specifying acid-free, neutral-sized paper
made from pulps which have not been elemental chlorine bleached. This pulp
is from farmed sustainable forests and was produced with special regard for
the environment.
Throughout, the printing and binding have been planned to ensure a sturdy,
attractive publication which should give years of enjoyment. If your copy fails
to meet our high standards, please inform us and we will gladly replace it.

Music Sales' complete catalogue describes thousands of
titles and is available in full colour sections by subject,
direct from Music Sales Limited.
Please state your areas of interest and send a
cheque/postal order for £1.50 for postage to:
Music Sales Limited, Newmarket Road, Bury St. Edmunds, Suffolk IP33 3YB.

www.musicsales.com

Saxophone Fingering Chart

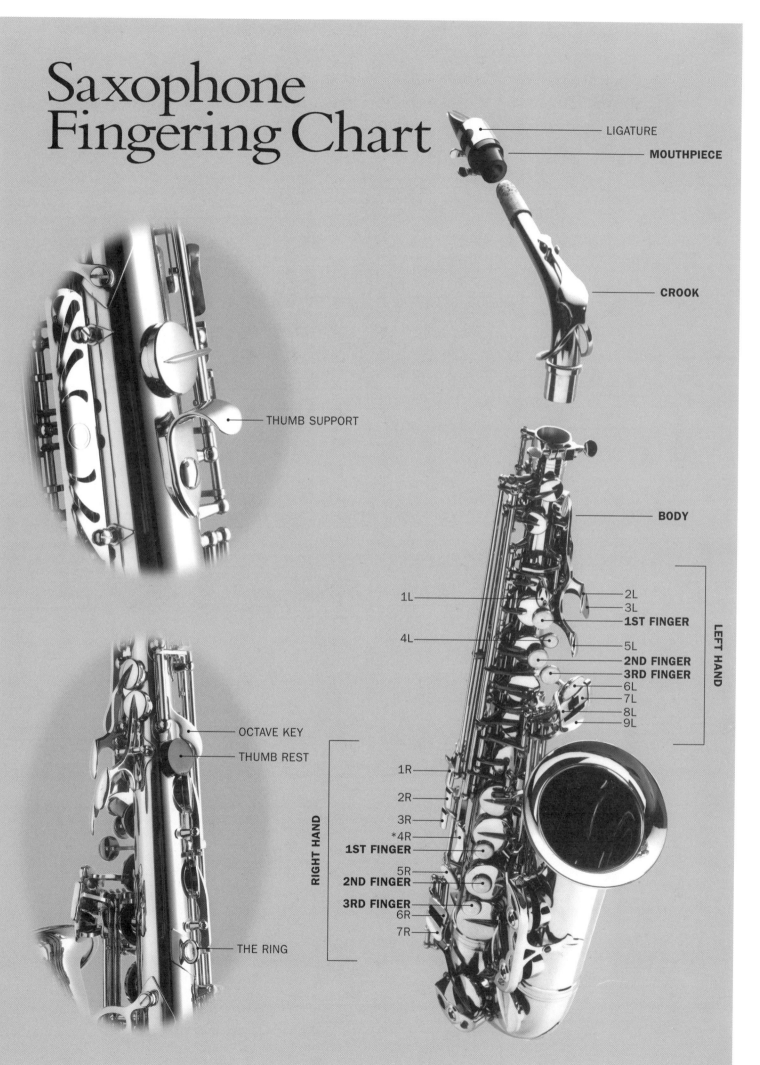

LIGATURE

MOUTHPIECE

CROOK

THUMB SUPPORT

BODY

1L

4L

2L
3L
1ST FINGER
5L
2ND FINGER
3RD FINGER
6L
7L
8L
9L

LEFT HAND

OCTAVE KEY

THUMB REST

RIGHT HAND

1R

2R

3R

*4R

1ST FINGER

5R

2ND FINGER

3RD FINGER

6R

7R

THE RING

* Not fitted on some saxophones

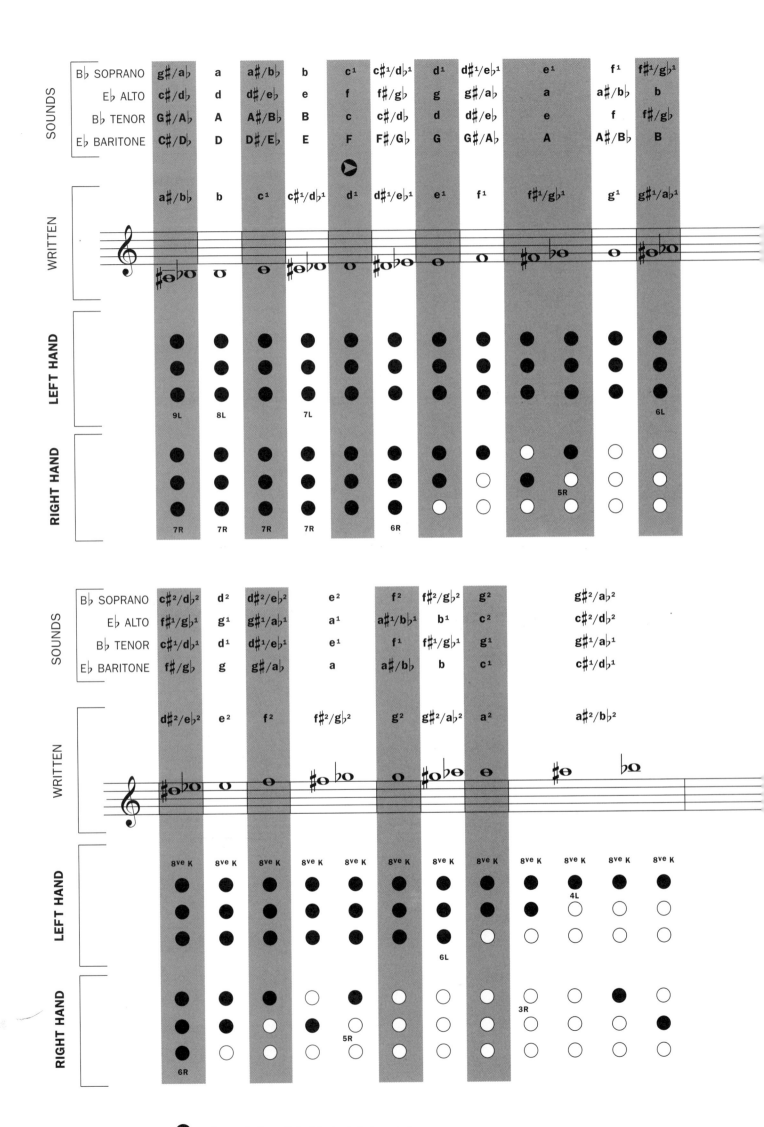

Indicates the lower limit of the best playing range

Indicates the upper limit of the best playing range

Fever #2.

Words & Music by John Davenport & Eddie Cooley

D. %: al Coda

CODA

Bésame Mucho #3.

Words & Music by Consuelo Velazquez

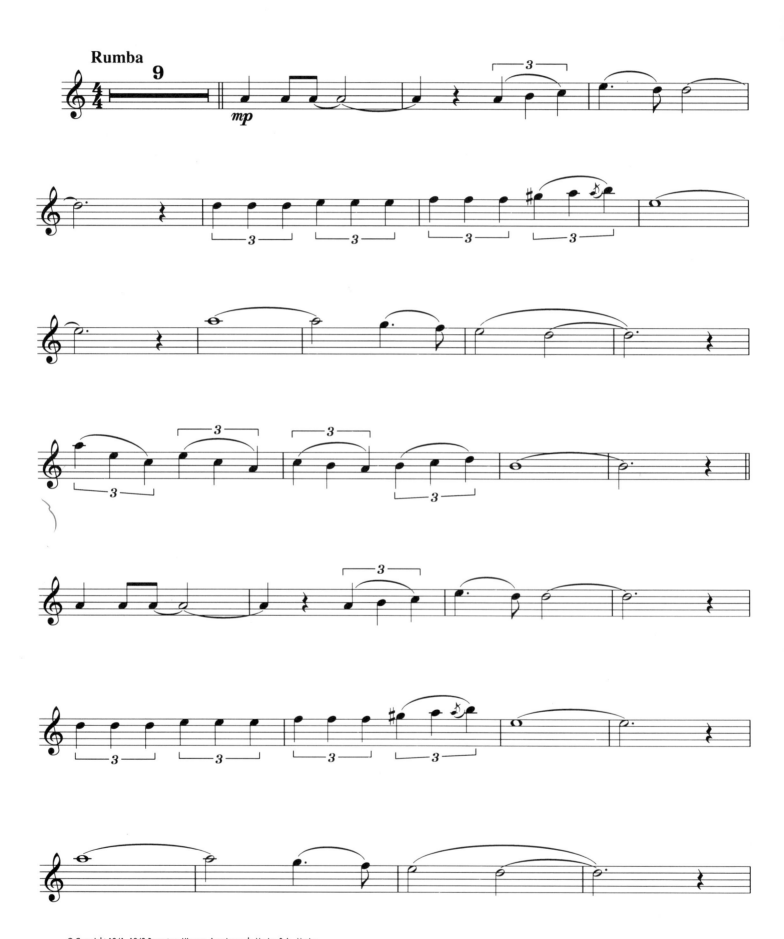

Fly Me To The Moon #4
(In Other Words)

Words & Music by Bart Howard

Medium fast (♩ = 88)

D.%: (with repeat) al Coda

⊕ CODA

God Bless' The Child #5

Words & Music by Arthur Herzog Jr. & Billie Holiday

Flying Home

By Benny Goodman & Lionel Hampton

#6.

Medium swing

Harlem Nocturne #7

Music by Earle Hagen
Words by Dick Rogers

Medium slow (♩ = 82)

rit.

Hit The Road Jack

Words & Music by Percy Mayfield

#8

Medium tempo (♩ = 126)

I Wish I Knew How
It Would Feel To Be Free #9

Music by Billy Taylor
Words by Billy Taylor & Dick Dallas

D. 𝄋 *al Coda*

CODA

Is You Is Or Is You Ain't My Baby?　#10.

Words & Music by Billy Austin & Louis Jordan

Moderate swing

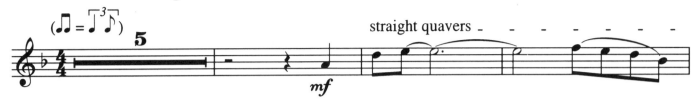

I'm Gettin' Sentimental Over You

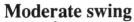

Music by George Bassman
Words by Ned Washington

Moderate swing

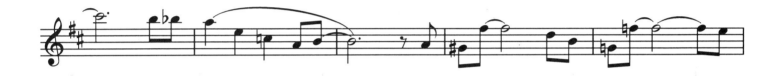

rall.

Jump, Jive An' Wail

#12.

Words & Music by Louis Prima

Bright swing

(straight quavers)

Li'l Darlin'

By Neal Hefti

#13.

Medium slow (♩ = 80)

To ⊕ *Coda*

D. 𝄋 al Coda

⊕ CODA

Mas Que Nada (Say No More) #14

Words & Music by Jorge Ben

Perdido

Music by Juan Tizol
Words by Harry Lenk and Ervin Drake

#15.

Perhaps, Perhaps, Perhaps
(Quizas, Quizas, Quizas)

#16.

Original Words & Music by Osvaldo Farres
English Words by Joe Davis

Satin Doll

Music by Duke Ellington & Billy Strayhorn
Words by Johnny Mercer

#17

Medium tempo ($\quad$ = 104)

To Coda

D.%. al Coda

$\oplus$ CODA

Straight No Chaser

#16.

By Thelonious Monk

Medium fast ($\quad$ = 80)

D.S. *(with repeat) al Coda*

CODA

Sway (Quien Sera) #19.

Original Words & Music by Pablo Beltran Ruiz
English Words by Norman Gimbel

Take The 'A' Train #20.

Words & Music by Billy Strayhorn

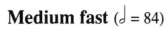

Medium fast ($\quad$ = 84)

To Coda

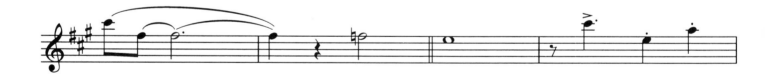

D.𝄋 (with repeats) al Coda

⊕ CODA

The Girl From Ipanema (Garota De Ipanema) #21

Music by Antonio Carlos Jobim
Original Words by Vinicius De Moraes
English Words by Norman Gimbel

Guest Spot

Play along with all your favourite music

Top line arrangements in each book. Hear full performance versions of the songs on the accompanying CD then play along with the recorded accompaniments.

ABBA

Includes: *Dancing Queen; Fernando; Mamma Mia; Waterloo.*

AM960905 Clarinet
AM960894 Flute
AM960916 Alto Saxophone
AM960927 Violin

BALLADS

Includes: *Candle In The Wind; Imagine; Killing Me Softly With His Song; Wonderful Tonight.*

AM941787 Clarinet
AM941798 Flute
AM941809 Alto Saxophone

THE BEATLES

Includes: *All You Need Is Love; Hey Jude; Lady Madonna; Yesterday.*

NO90682 Clarinet
NO90683 Flute
NO90684 Alto Saxophone

CHART HITS

Includes: *Baby One More Time (Britney Spears); Bring It All Back (S Club 7); That Don't Impress Me Much (Shania Twain); When You Say Nothing At All (Ronan Keating).*

AM955636 Clarinet
AM955647 Flute
AM955658 Alto Saxophone
AM966724 Violin

CHRISTMAS

Includes: *Frosty The Snowman; Have Yourself A Merry Little Christmas; Mary's Boy Child; Winter Wonderland.*

AM950400 Clarinet
AM950411 Flute
AM950422 Alto Saxophone

CHRISTMAS HITS

Includes: *Happy Christmas (War Is Over); I Wish It Could Be Christmas Every Day; Merry Christmas Everybody; Mistletoe And Wine.*

AM966955 Clarinet
AM966944 Flute
AM966966 Alto Saxophone
AM966977 Violin

CLASSIC BLUES

Includes: *Cry Me A River; Moonglow; Round Midnight; Swingin' Shepherd Blues.*

AM941743 Clarinet
AM941754 Flute
AM941765 Alto Saxophone
AM966702 Tenor Saxophone
AM967048 Trumpet

CLASSICS

Includes: *Air On The 'G' String - Bach; Jupiter (from The Planets Suite) - Holst; Ode To Joy (Theme from Symphony No.9 'Choral') - Beethoven; Swan Lake (Theme) - Tchaikovsky.*

AM955537 Clarinet
AM955548 Flute
AM955560 Violin

FILM THEMES

Includes: *Circle Of Life (The Lion King); Kiss From A Rose (Batman Forever); Moon River (Breakfast At Tiffany's); You Must Love Me (Evita).*

AM941864 Clarinet
AM941875 Flute
AM941886 Alto Saxophone

JAZZ

Includes: *Fly Me To The Moon; Opus One; Satin Doll; Straight No Chaser.*

AM941700 Clarinet
AM941710 Flute
AM941721 Alto Saxophone
AM966779 Tenor Saxophone
AM966691 Trumpet

LATIN

Includes: *Dos Gardenias; The Girl From Ipanema; Guantanamera; Lambada.*

AM966064 Clarinet
AM966053 Flute
AM966075 Alto Saxophone
AM967758 Trumpet

NINETIES HITS

Includes: *Falling Into You (Celine Dion); Never Ever (All Saints); Tears In Heaven (Eric Clapton); 2 Become 1 (Spice Girls).*

AM952853 Clarinet
AM952864 Flute
AM952875 Alto Saxophone
AM966713 Violin

No.1 HITS

Includes: *A Whiter Shade Of Pale (Procol Harum); Every Breath You Take (The Police); No Matter What (Boyzone); Unchained Melody (The Righteous Brothers).*

AM955603 Clarinet
AM955614 Flute
AM955625 Alto Saxophone
AM959530 Violin

SHOWSTOPPERS

Includes: *Big Spender (Sweet Charity); Bring Him Home (Les Misérables); I Know Him So Well (Chess); Somewhere (West Side Story).*

AM941820 Clarinet
AM941831 Flute
AM941842 Alto Saxophone

SMASH HITS

Includes: *American Pie (Madonna); I Have A Dream (Westlife); Pure Shores (All Saints); She's The One (Robbie Williams).*

AM963040 Clarinet
AM963039 Flute
AM963050 Alto Saxophone
AM968209 Violin

SWING

Includes: *Flying Home; Swing That Music; Tuxedo Junction; Zoot Suit Riot.*

AM949377 Clarinet
AM949399 Alto Saxophone
AM959618 Tenor Saxophone
AM960575 Trumpet

TV THEMES

Includes: *Black Adder; Home And Away; London's Burning; Star Trek.*

AM941908 Clarinet
AM941919 Flute
AM941920 Alto Saxophone

GOLD EDITION

Double-CD bumper compilation. Twenty all-time hit songs, showstoppers and film themes.

AM960729 Clarinet
AM960718 Flute
AM960730 Alto Saxophone

PLATINUM EDITION

Double-CD bumper compilation. Seventeen greatest chart hits, ballads and film themes.

AM960751 Clarinet
AM960740 Flute
AM960762 Alto Saxophone

Available from good music retailers, or in case of difficulty, contact:
Music Sales Limited, Newmarket Road, Bury St. Edmunds, Suffolk IP33 3YB.
Tel: 01284 725725; Fax: 01284 702592. www.musicsales.com

Great Clarendon Street, Oxford OX2 6DP, England
198 Madison Avenue, New York, NY10016, USA

Oxford is a registered trade mark of Oxford University Press
in the UK and in certain other countries

ISBN 0–19–321061–4   978–0–19–321061–5

Acknowledgements
The publisher is grateful for permission to reproduce the following poem:

Kaye Umansky: 'The Wolf's Tale' from *Nonsense Animal Rhymes* by Kaye Umansky (OUP, 2001),
by permission of Oxford University Press.